Sterling Publishers Private Limited
A-59, Okhla Ind. Area, Phase II, New Delhi-110020. India
Tel: 91-11-26386165; Fax: 91-11-26383788
E-mail: sterlingpublishers@airtelmail.in
Website: www.sterlingpublishers.com

Printed at Sterling Publishers Pvt. Ltd, New Delhi

The Invincible
Hanuman

Foreword

Retold through centuries in time, this is the story of the strong and mighty Hanuman – the greatest devotee of Lord Ram and the most valiant and loyal of all his soldiers. Born on earth as an incarnation of Lord Shiva, and as the godson of Pawan Dev, the god of wind, Hanuman was endowed by the gods with the gifts of immortality, invincibility and wisdom.

He stands as one of the most popular gods of Hindu mythology. This book narrates the tales of Hanuman as a playful and mischievous child, and later as he grows up to become one of the world's most heroic and noble figures.

Hanuman represents strength, wisdom and devotion. His devotion to Lord Ram was remarkable as he journeyed across the ocean, conquering all obstacles in his way to find Mother Sita. Out of all his feats, he is most remembered for his quest in search of the *Sanjivani* herb where he carried an entire mountain to Lanka!

Journey with us as we take you through the world of Hanuman and his adventures!

Contents

Birth of Hanuman

A long time ago, in the kingdom of heaven, there lived an *apsara* called Punjikasthala. She served Vrihaspati, the guru of Gods.

One day, Vrihaspati became really angry at Punjikasthala because she disobeyed him.

"You shall be born on earth as a female monkey!" he cursed her.

"Oh! Please take that curse back," begged Punjikasthala, but the sage, still angry at the *apsara*, refused to listen and walked away.

Punjikasthala was worried that the curse might come true, so she quickly went up to Lord Brahma.

"Lord Brahma, I have been cursed by the guru of Gods, Vrihaspati! Please have mercy and lift the curse!" she begged.

Lord Brahma listened to her story and took pity on her.

"You shall be the blessed mother of the incarnation of Lord Shiva on earth. The sage's curse would be lifted after that," assured Lord Brahma.

9

So, as it had been foretold, the *apsara* was born on earth as a beautiful monkey called Anjana. Kesari, the bravest and the strongest of the monkeys was struck by her beauty. Tales of his courage were known to all. When the two met, they immediately fell in love and got married.

After the marriage, Anjana remembered Lord Brahma's promise, and so, she prayed to Lord Shiva. Lord Shiva heard her prayers and appeared before her. He blessed her and said, "You shall soon bear my human incarnation on earth."

Around the same time, at the bank of the River Sarayu, King Dashratha of Ayodhya was also performing a *yajna* in order to have children. Out of the holy fire of the *yajna-kund*, a divine figure appeared with a bowl of *kheer*. He asked Dashratha to give the divine *kheer* to his three queens.

As Dashratha was giving a bowl of *kheer* to one of his queens, a kite swooped down and snatched the bowl of *kheer* and flew away.

14

While flying over the forests where Anjana and Kesari lived, the kite dropped the bowl of *kheer*. Pawan Dev, the god of wind blew and dropped the divine portion right on to Anjana's lap.

Anjana believed it to be God's blessing and ate it. She was soon going to give birth to Lord Shiva's incarnation.

A few months before the baby was born, Bali, the king of monkeys had a dream. In that dream, he saw that a monkey named Anjana would soon bear a child who would be the strongest on the planet, stronger than Bali himself. Bali became very jealous and ordered his guards to kill the child in Anjana's womb.

He immediately sent his guards to Anjana's home and while she was sleeping, they shot an arrow at her. However, when the arrow pierced through Anjana's belly, it turned into gold earrings for the child inside!

Anjana too, remained unhurt and within a few days, she bore a beautiful monkey boy with an innocent face and large intelligent eyes.

This was the birth of Hanuman.

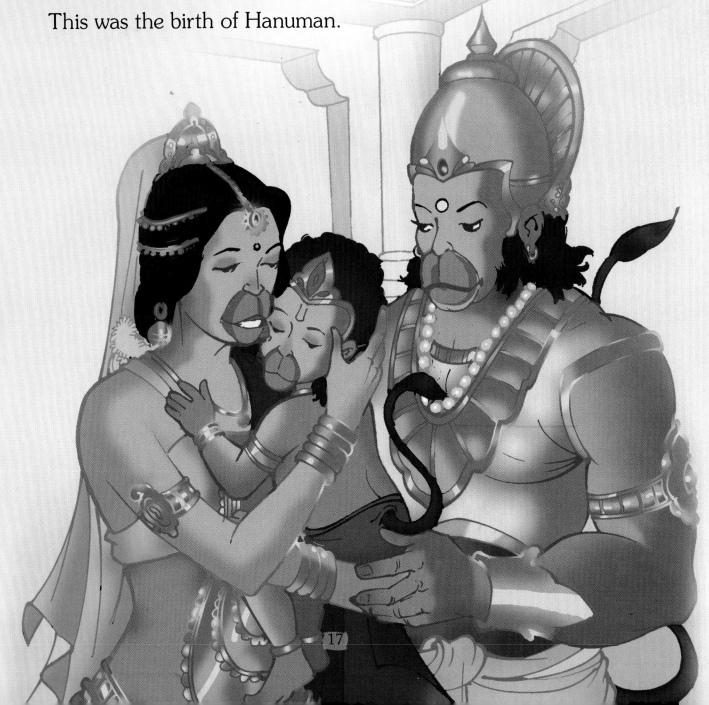

Hanuman's Childhood

Kesari and Anjana were very fond of their child, so much that Hanuman turned out to be a very naughty child. He was stronger than any child of his age. He was swifter than air and he could leap through unbelievably long distances. He could uproot trees and fight with wild elephants. He was always out with his friends, playing and jumping from one treetop to another.

One day, Hanuman was playing with his mother. Anjana asked him to sit down and told him that it was time for her to go back to heaven. Little Hanuman didn't understand what his mother meant.

He asked, "Mother, are you going somewhere? Take me with you!"

Anjana smiled, "Son, you cannot go there just yet. I have to return home. I was born on earth only to be your blessed mother."

20

Hanuman started crying and then innocently asked his mother, "But mother, if you go away, who will give me food? Who will love me?"

Anjana said, "You are a special child, Hanuman. You don't know that yet but the whole universe will love you forever! And just look around you, nature is abundant. She'll provide you with food when I am not around."

Saying this, Anjana left Hanuman and returned to her home in heaven.

One hot day, little Hanuman had been playing with his friends. He felt very hungry and remembered his mother's words. He looked around to see if he could find anything to eat. Suddenly, he saw a red coloured apple hanging in the sky. It was the sun!

But innocent Hanuman believed it to be food that Mother Nature had put out for him. Instantly, he leapt towards it. He was surprised to find that the fruit was much farther than he had expected! So, he kept on flying towards it.

When Rahu saw that a monkey child was about to swallow the sun, he panicked. He ran to Indra, the king of Gods and said, "A monkey child is going to eat the sun!"

When Indra heard that somebody was entering his kingdom of heaven without his permission, he grew furious and set out fully armed. As soon as he saw Hanuman, he flung his mighty weapon, the *Vajra,* at the poor child. The mighty weapon hit him hard on his chin (*hanu*) and made a permanent mark on it. This is how Hanuman got his name.

The mighty blow from the *Vajra* hurt Hanuman and he fell down upon the earth, unconscious.

25

Pawan Dev, the God of Wind, was furious at this brutal treatment of his godson. He stopped blowing completely. Then he took Hanuman's unconscious body and stormed away to *Patal Lok* (the under-world). The entire earth became helpless without air. All living beings began to die!

Fearing Pawan Dev's wrath, the gods accompanied by the trinity of the Lords Brahma, Vishnu and Shiva descended to the under-world. They revived Hanuman who sat up quickly and watched them all with blinking eyes. Pawan Dev, the God of Wind, was happy to see his godson up and about. He started blowing again and the entire creation heaved a sigh of relief.

One by one, the gods blessed the unique child. Lord Brahma spoke, "You shall remain invincible. No weapon including my *Brahmaastra* shall be able to overpower you."

Lord Vishnu spoke, "You shall be my greatest devotee. Ages to come shall be reminded of your selfless devotion."

Kuber gave Hanuman a mace that could not be beaten by any other in the entire creation.

Yamraj, the God of Death, said, "Death shall never be able to touch you."

Surya dev, the Sun God, said, "I give one-hundredth of my power to you. I impart to you the power by the virtue of which you shall be able to assume the smallest and the largest forms."

So spoke all the gods and blessed Hanuman. Hanuman became the most powerful and most intelligent living being ever!

Days went by and Hanuman continued to grow naughty. He had become extremely powerful but was too young to be able to control his power. He would jump from one treetop to another, run around the entire forest and play with wild tigers. He would disturb sages in their worship in order to make them play with him! He ran away with their rosaries and holy books and hid them in the forest. Innocently, little Hanuman ended up causing a lot of trouble to the sages. They tried to persuade him to control himself but Hanuman would not listen.

Finally, the sages couldn't take it anymore.

One day, they said, "Hanuman! You are too powerful for your own good! You have been misusing your powers to disrupt forest life. We curse you that from this day on, you shall forget the extent of your powers! You will remember them only when somebody reminds you about them."

The next instant, Hanuman forgot all his powers! He grew sober and thoughtful. The forest became serene and peaceful again.

Hanuman's Education

In a few years, Hanuman grew up and decided to find the meaning of his life. The Sun God was considered to know everything in life as he had been there since the beginning of time. He moves around the earth and sees everything. When Hanuman expressed his wish to be his student, the Sun God refused.

He said, "I have to be constantly moving. If I stop, the universe will collapse. It will be impossible for you to learn from me this way." Then the Sun God disappeared.

But Hanuman was adamant to have the Sun God as his teacher. So, he joined his palms and began praying.

Soon he began expanding in size! He grew bigger and bigger and bigger until he could touch the stars and the planets. Then he placed one foot over the Himalayas and the other over the ocean on the opposite side.

He turned towards the Sun and said, "I shall not rest until I have learnt from you. Since you cannot stop, I shall keep moving along with you!"

The Sun God was very pleased with Hanuman's dedication. He blessed him and accepted him as his student. Hanuman was a very keen and fast learner.

After his education had been completed, Hanuman offered to give him *guru-dakshina*, but the Sun God refused. However, when Hanuman insisted, the god asked him to take care of Sugriva, the prince of the monkeys. Hanuman happily agreed and took leave of his teacher.

Hanuman helps Sugriva

One day a mighty demon called Mayawi came to Kishkindha and challenged Bali to a fight. Bali accepted. A terrifying battle ensued between the two as they were both well-matched in strength. It went on for days. Sugriva and the ministers grew worried.

Suddenly, in the middle of the fight, Mayawi ran back to his cave and Bali followed him. He was about to enter it when Sugriva too came running behind him.

He said, "Brother, don't go inside! It's his cave. He might play some trick on you."

But Bali didn't listen to him. He replied, "I have to finish the fight. I will destroy this demon and come out within fifteen days. Wait for me here!" Saying this, Bali entered the cave.

Fifteen days passed. Sugriva waited at the entrance but Bali didn't come out. Sugriva became very worried. He wondered what to do next. One day, he saw a stream of blood flowing out from that cave! He thought that his brother Bali had been killed by Mayawi. He rushed to the nearest boulder and put it against the cave door so that the demon would not be able to come out again. Then with a heavy heart, he returned to Kishkindha.

He grieved for his brother for days. But the kingdom needed a ruler. On the ministers' insistence, he accepted the crown and became the king of Kishkindha.

However, it was Bali who had defeated the powerful Mayawi! It was the demon's blood that Sugriva had seen flowing out of the cave.

After killing him, Bali too was injured and tired to walk out of the cave. He rested inside the cave for sometime.

Finally when he made his way to the entrance of the cave, he found it blocked! He grew furious! He knew it was his brother who had blocked it. He suspected that perhaps it was because Sugriva wanted the throne for himself.

He struggled with the heavy boulder for days until one day, he managed to push it aside.

Fuming, Bali reached Kishkindha where he found his brother enthroned. Sugriva was pleasantly surprised to see his brother alive.

He rushed to meet him but Bali spoke out in a thundering voice, "Traitor! I loved you so much and this is how you have repaid me! You had put that boulder on the entrance of the cave because you did not want me to return to my kingdom. You wanted the throne for yourself! I shall punish you duly!"

Sugriva tried to explain the matter to his brother but Bali was too angry to pay any heed to what he had to say. He drove him out of the kingdom and snatched away his wife, Ruma.

Around this time, Sugriva received Hanuman's support who was sent to protect him in his exile.

Hanuman suggested Sugriva to move to Rishyamukha Mountain as he knew that due to a curse, Bali couldn't go there. Sugriva was grateful for Hanuman's advice. He made Hanuman his minister and chief advisor.

This is how Hanuman begins his journey – by serving the banished king Sugriva.

45

Hanuman meets the Prince of Ayodhya

Away from Hanuman and Sugriva at the Rishyamukha Mountain, during the same time, there also lived a strong and valiant prince by the name of Ram. His mother also partook of the divine *kheer* as did Hanuman's mother.

Ram was married to Sita, the beautiful princess of Mithila in her *swayamvar*. But Kaikeyi, Ram's stepmother, asked him to go away for a fourteen year exile so that her son Bharat could sit on the throne of Ayodhya. Ram along with Sita and brother Lakshman spent the exile in various forests.

Once, while they were staying at a beautiful place called Panchavati, a *rakshasi* called Shurpanakha was passing by the forest. She was the sister of Ravana, the king of the golden Lanka. She was allured by Ram's personality and fell in love with him, immediately.

She took the form of a beautiful maiden and approached him.

"Your attractive looks have cast a spell on me. Come with me and be my husband," said Shurpanakha.

Ram replied, "O noble lady, I am a married man and this is Sita my beloved wife. I cannot be your husband."

When Shurpanakha heard these words, she became very angry. Overcome with jealousy, she changed back to her original *rakshasi* form and charged towards Sita with hateful eyes, "You ugly mortal, I shall kill you and eat you up!"

Sita got frightened and stepped back. However, Lakshman grew furious. In a fit of rage, he took out his dagger and cut off Shurpanakha's nose!

Screaming and howling with pain, she dashed back to her brother, Ravana. When Ravana saw his sister in that state, he was enraged. Shurpanakha told him the whole story and begged him to take revenge. She also added that Sita was the most beautiful woman she had ever seen and that she was fit to be only Ravana's wife.

Ravana decided to abduct Sita to avenge his sister's humiliation.

He asked Mareecha, a demon, to transform himself into a golden deer. Ravana explained the whole plan to the demon and set out for Panchavati. When he reached Panchavati, Mareecha in the form of a golden deer, began prancing around in front of Ram and Sita's hut, just as Ravana had instructed. Sita saw this magnificent deer and was captivated by its beauty. She requested Ram to bring the deer for her so that she could keep it as a pet. Ram asked Lakshman to take care of Sita and set out in search of it.

Mareecha led Ram far away from the hut. When Ram got close to it, he sensed something strange about the deer. So, he shot an arrow right through the deer's heart. Just as the arrow hit him, he transformed back to his original form and cried out, in a voice exactly like Ram's, "O Sita! O Lakshman!"

Thinking that Ram was in trouble, Lakshman rushed to help him, leaving Sita alone in the hut.

Ravana, taking full advantage of the situation, appeared and took Sita on to his chariot and made his way back to Lanka.

Jatayu, the king of vultures, heard Sita's cries and tried to free her from Ravana, but Ravana sliced off his wings and he fell to the ground.

Ram and Lakshman were too late to rescue her and by the time they reached, Sita was already gone. There they found Jatayu.

"It was Ravana, king of the demons who took your queen, My Lord," said the vulture who was breathing his last. Ram and Lakshman tried to search for her everywhere but to no avail.

On their way, they met a cursed *rakshasa*, Kabandh, whose body parts had been interchanged so that his mouth was on his belly and his eyes on his chest. Ram and Lakshman freed him from the curse. He had been cursed for harassing the sages and was told that it would be lifted by Ram, the prince of Ayodhya.

In return for the deed, Kabandh asked Ram and Lakshman, "What brings you here? Perhaps I could help you with something?"

When he heard their story he warned the two that Ravana was very powerful and it would be difficult to invade his kingdom.

"You should get a powerful ally if you want to defeat Ravana. Go to the Rishyamukha Mountains and seek Sugriva. You shall be able to help each other," advised Kabandh.

58

Back at the Rishyamukha Mountains, Hanuman was still there acting as Sugriva's chief advisor. One day, they saw two armed men coming towards them. Hanuman sped down to the foot of the mountain and transformed himself into a Brahmin.

When he met them, he asked them what brought them to the mountain. Ram replied, "We have come to meet Sugriva. We need his help."

But, as Ram spoke, Hanuman suddenly recognised who he was and fell down at his feet with reverence.

Hanuman immediately led the two to Sugriva. When Sugriva found out that the two young men were the Ayodhya princes Ram and Lakshman, he received them most cordially.

Both Ram and Sugriva shared their stories with each other. Sugriva promised that he would assemble all monkeys of the world and set them in search of Sita. Ram too offered to help him against Bali.

Hanuman lit a fire and the two friends pledged to support each other.

The following day, Ram set out with Sugriva towards Kishkindha. There, he shot Bali with an arrow and killed him. Once Bali was killed, Sugriva was crowned the king of Kishkindha.

Hanuman helps to find Sita

Now that he was the king of the monkeys, Sugriva could help Ram defeat Ravana and bring back Sita. He asked Hanuman to assemble all the monkeys before him. Hanuman assembled monkeys of every kind, from all over the world. He delivered such a moving speech that even Ram admired his skill.

Sugriva sent the monkeys in all directions. He said, "Search for Mother Sita. I give you all a month's time. Come back with news about mother Sita or don't return at all!"

So the monkeys set out in large numbers in search of Sita. Before leaving, Hanuman took the blessings of Ram. Ram looked at him kindly and took out his signet ring with 'Ram' engraved on it.

Ram said, "I am sure you will be successful, Hanuman. I have complete faith in you. Give this ring to Sita when you see her. She will recognise you as my messenger and will receive you kindly." Hanuman took the ring with due honour and joined the others for the journey.

They kept moving southwards for days. But they got no clue regarding Sita's whereabouts. One month was about to get over. The monkeys were in great despair. Then a vulture called Sampati passed by and asked what the matter was. Hanuman told him the story of how Ravana abducted Sita and he decided to help them against the demon. He was old but he still had a very keen eye-sight.

He looked across the wide ocean and spoke to them all, "Across the ocean lies the golden city of Lanka. Ravana, the ten-headed demon, reigns there. In a lovely garden located inside Ravana's palace, I can see a beautiful but a sad looking woman. She must be the one whom you all seek."

Hanuman in Lanka

The monkeys were overjoyed. They thanked Sampati. But the joy proved to be short-lived. The task that lay ahead of them was to cross the mighty ocean in front of them! They didn't have a flying chariot like Ravana!

Hanuman was still under the curse that he had got from the sages in his childhood so he was unaware of his powers.

Jambavanta spoke, "O valiant son of wind, you are the mightiest of us all. None can rival your valour, strength and splendour! Expand yourself, O Hanuman! And leap over the entire ocean!"

Hanuman was immediately reminded of his powers and began to expand in size. He attained his full strength and started towering over the mountains.

As the gigantic figure of Hanuman took flight above the vast ocean, the gods and other celestial beings rained flowers upon him. The sun did not burn him and the wind soothed him. The Ocean too decided to help him.

Now he could see the golden city on the horizon. He shrunk his size so that the guards in Lanka couldn't spot him.

Soon, he reached Lanka. At night the golden city gleamed under the moonlight. Hanuman thought, "The city of Lanka is rightly compared with the city of Gods. It is as splendid as the abode of Gods above."

He reached the city gates where a demon called Lankini stood guarding the entire city. When she tried to stop him, Hanuman challenged her to a fight. Hanuman defeated her easily.

Lankini said, "I had once been told that the day I would be defeated by a monkey, it would herald the end of Ravana and Lanka. It seems that the time has come."

Thus saying, she let Hanuman enter Lanka.

Hanuman looked around, and in the middle of the Ashoka Garden, saw a beautiful but sad-looking woman sitting under an Ashoka tree. She was surrounded by armed *rakshasis*. Hanuman recognised Sita at once.

70

Having reduced his size, he perched on the tree under which Sita sat and waited there for the right moment to reveal himself to her. The *rakshasis* were tormenting her with their poisonous words. Suddenly, Ravana entered the garden with his followers.

He said, "I know it is not sensible on my part to be asking another man's wife to be mine. But I am captivated by your beauty. Be mine or face death!" Sita was firm and refused. Ravana became furious. He gave her two month's time to change her mind and stormed out.

As the night drew on, the *rakshasis* went to sleep. Sita was full of sorrow and despair. At that moment, Hanuman began to sing Ram's story in a sweet voice. She understood that the singer was a friend of Ram and asked him to appear before her.

Hanuman instantly jumped down from the tree. Changing back to his original size, he bowed down in front of her and said, "Mother Sita, I come here as a messenger from Lord Ram. Ram is well but worried about your well-being. His soothing words comforted Sita and he presented her with Ram's ring.

Hanuman told Sita that seeing how she was being treated there, he couldn't leave her behind. But Sita said, "Hanuman, I know it's easy for you to carry me out of Lanka. But my husband's respect is at stake too. He must defeat Ravana and then take me away with due honour." Hanuman understood.

Sita then pulled out the *churamani*, the jewel that she wore in her hair and gave it to Hanuman saying, "Give this to Ram, Hanuman!" Hanuman took it and left.

Before leaving, Hanuman decided to destroy the city of Lanka to teach Ravana a lesson. He expanded in size and began to uproot trees and pillars. The sleeping demons of Lanka woke up with a start and saw Hanuman run riot. He had become larger than giants and looked ferocious to his enemies. The demon army began attacking Hanuman. Hanuman defeated all of them easily.

The uproar reached Ravana's ears. He ordered his son Aksha to go and bring the giant monkey to him. Aksha owned a strong chariot which he had received from the gods, drawn by eight beautiful horses. When Hanuman saw him, he headed straight towards him. In one blow, Hanuman broke the splendid chariot into pieces. Aksha jumped to the ground and challenged Hanuman. Hanuman struck a mighty blow at Aksha. The next instant, Ravana's son lay dead. Ravana was enraged to hear of Aksha's death. He turned to his other son Indrajit. Indrajit was a very courageous warrior. He had once defeated Indra, the king of the gods.

Ravana said, "You are amongst the best warriors equipped with celestial weapons. Go and bring this monkey to me!" Indrajit set out to seek Hanuman. He could see the giant figure of Hanuman from a distance. He chose the most fatal arrows from his quiver and attacked Hanuman. But to his surprise, the mighty monkey just brushed them aside! Now Hanuman rushed towards Indrajit.

Indrajit evoked his celestial weapons and attacked Hanuman but he still could not harm him. Indrajit knew that he had no other option but to use his invincible weapon, the *Brahmaastra*, given to him by Lord Brahma. Indrajit struck the weapon at Hanuman.

When Hanuman realised that the *Brahmaastra* had been unleashed at him, he surrendered to its power out of respect for Lord Brahma, the creator of the universe.

Although Hanuman could have easily set himself free when Indrajit tied him up, he did not do so as he wanted to see Ravana.

Indrajit, Hanuman and the demon army reached the king's palace. Hanuman changed back to his original size. He was brought before Ravana in his court. Hanuman saw Ravana sitting atop his magnificent crystal throne studded with the rarest diamonds and pearls. Even Hanuman was impressed with the brilliance.

"O disrespectful monkey, tell us who has sent you here?" asked Ravana.

"I am a messenger of Lord Ram. Restore mother Sita to Lord Ram with due honour and ask for his forgiveness if you want to save yourself and your clan" replied Hanuman.

Angry at such words, Ravana said, "How dare you talk to the ten-headed demon king like that? You shall soon know why even gods tremble at the mention of my name!" He ordered Hanuman to be killed immediately.

Vibhishana, Ravana's younger brother, was a wise and learned man. He was a devotee of Lord Ram himself. He interrupted and told Ravana that it was not proper to kill a messenger. Ravana agreed and said, "Then we won't kill this monkey. But he must be punished. A monkey's tail is the most prized part of his body. Set his tail on fire and let him go!" Saying this, Ravana laughed.

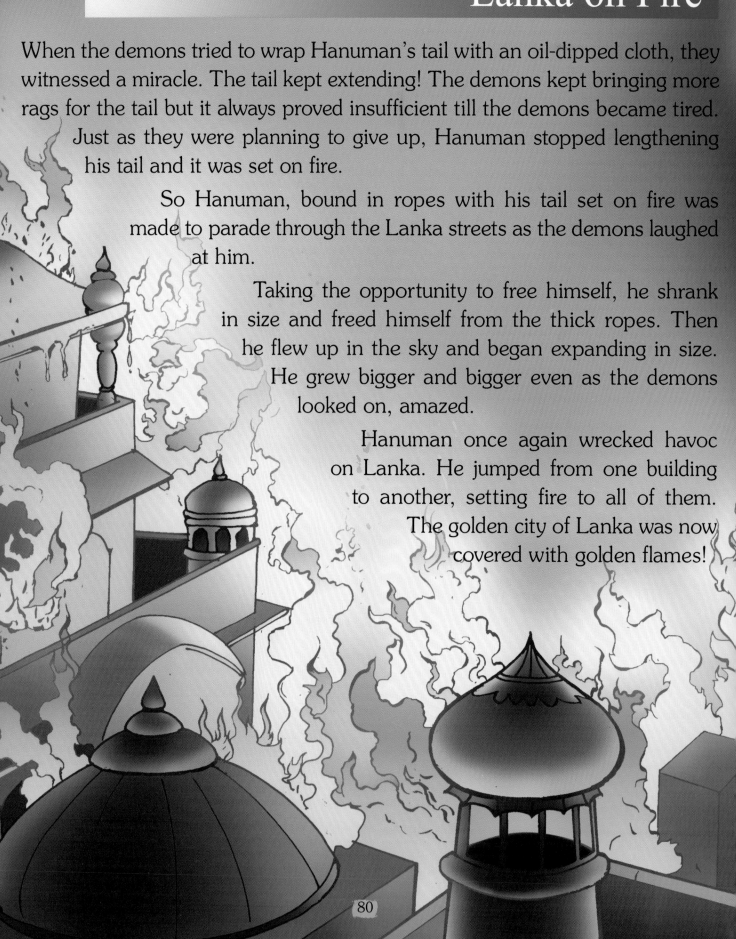

Lanka on Fire

When the demons tried to wrap Hanuman's tail with an oil-dipped cloth, they witnessed a miracle. The tail kept extending! The demons kept bringing more rags for the tail but it always proved insufficient till the demons became tired. Just as they were planning to give up, Hanuman stopped lengthening his tail and it was set on fire.

So Hanuman, bound in ropes with his tail set on fire was made to parade through the Lanka streets as the demons laughed at him.

Taking the opportunity to free himself, he shrank in size and freed himself from the thick ropes. Then he flew up in the sky and began expanding in size. He grew bigger and bigger even as the demons looked on, amazed.

Hanuman once again wrecked havoc on Lanka. He jumped from one building to another, setting fire to all of them. The golden city of Lanka was now covered with golden flames!

Having done this, Hanuman dipped his tail in the ocean to put the fire out and then he set off on the journey back. He leapt across the ocean till he landed among the monkeys who were eagerly awaiting his arrival. They were happy to see Hanuman come back from the mission, safe.

Hanuman informed them about Sita's well-being. Then, he told them all that had happened to him in Lanka. They were all awestruck at his valour!

Hanuman and others returned to Ram, Lakshman and Sugriva. When Hanuman gave Ram the jewel that Sita sent, he was relieved to know that she was alive. But he was sad to hear of her unhappiness. He knew that they needed to act fast.

Building a Bridge

Now as they knew exactly where Sita was being held captive, the preparations for the battle started at Sugriva's command. But a huge problem still remained. The ocean lay between them and Lanka, and to get the whole army to cross it would be a very difficult task.

They then asked for help from the Ocean God who told Ram that Nala (the son of Vishwakarma, the architect of gods) could build a bridge across the ocean. He was a part of the monkey army. Nala began to build the bridge with the help of the other monkeys. They carried huge boulders, rocks and trees to the ocean and dropped them into the water. Hanuman wrote the name of 'Ram' on each one of them to make them float on the surface. Soon, the bridge was constructed and Ram's army marched off towards Lanka.

Quest for Sanjivani

Hanuman was set to destroy the demon army and he thrashed several of them at one go. Meanwhile, Ram and Lakshman fought with the demon warriors. One by one, they defeated all the army generals of Ravana's army. Ravana was enraged. He sent his valiant son, Indrajit, to the battlefield. But Lakshman killed him too with the help of Vibhishana and Hanuman.

When Ravana heard the news, he entered the battle himself and headed towards Lakshman and hurled a fatal spear at him. Lakshman fell down unconscious. When Ram, Hanuman and others saw this, they rushed towards Lakshman's motionless body.

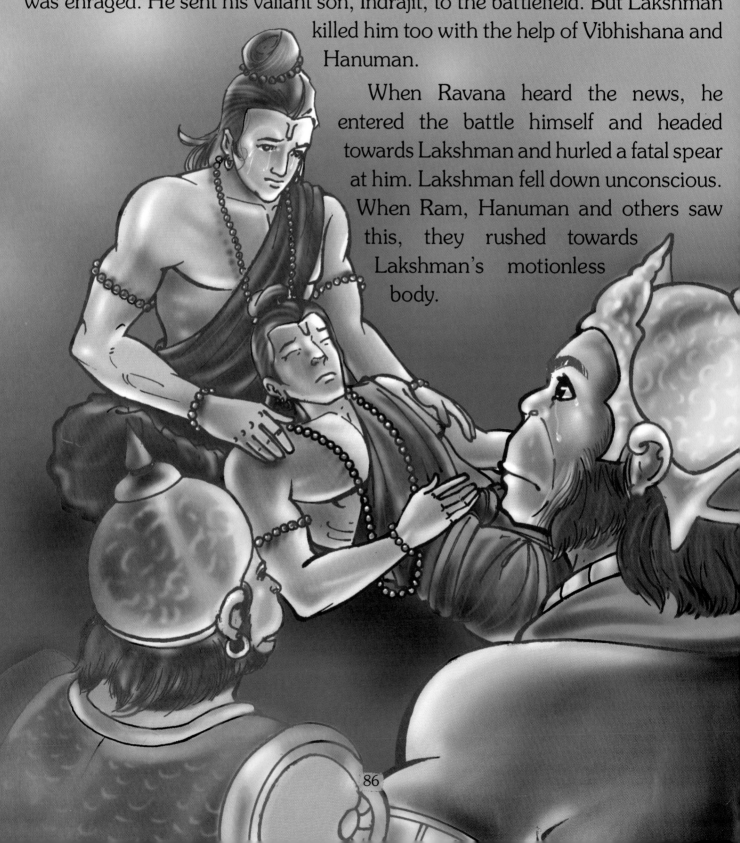

Susena, the physician, examined Lakshman and told Ram that he was still alive. Then he addressed Hanuman, "Mighty son of wind, go to the southern peak of the Himalayas. Bring me the *Sanjivani* herb which has medicinal qualities."

As soon as Hanuman heard this, he set off towards the Himalayas. But when he reached that peak, he couldn't recognise the herb.

Hanuman wondered what could be done as every moment was precious. He decided to carry the entire mountain along with him! He expanded in size and towered over the Himalayas. Then he lifted the mountain and flew back to the battlefield.

Everyone was overjoyed to see Hanuman approaching with the entire mountain. The Gods too blessed Hanuman. Susena quickly selected the herbs he needed to treat Lakshman and the battle was resumed.

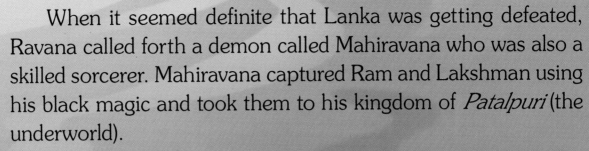

When it seemed definite that Lanka was getting defeated, Ravana called forth a demon called Mahiravana who was also a skilled sorcerer. Mahiravana captured Ram and Lakshman using his black magic and took them to his kingdom of *Patalpuri* (the underworld).

Hanuman followed the sorcerer. But when Hanuman reached the gates of *Patalpuri*, he saw that a strange creature was guarding them. The creature was half fish and half monkey! He was called Makardhwaja. He told Hanuman that he was his son. Hanuman was surprised and asked him to narrate his story.

Makardhwaja told him that after setting Lanka on fire, when Hanuman had dipped his tail in the ocean to put it out, a drop of his sweat fell into the ocean. That's how he was born.

Makardhwaja took blessings from his father but said that he must fight him because guarding the gates of *Patalpuri* was his duty which must be fulfilled. Hanuman fought with his son and defeated him. Then he tied him up and went inside.

Hanuman entered Mahiravana's palace. He came to know that in order to kill him, he had to put off five lamps at the same time! Hanuman thought for a while as to how it could be done. Then Hanuman assumed a *panchmukha* form (*Panch-mukha* means five faces) and blew out the five lamps simultaneously.

Mahiravana was thus killed by Hanuman. Hanuman freed Ram and Lakshman. Before leaving, they crowned Hanuman's son Makardhwaja as the king of *Patalpuri*. Hanuman blessed his son and advised him to rule with generosity and wisdom.

The end of Ravana

After returning from *Patalpuri*, they headed to the battlefield. Ram decided that it was time he fought the final battle with Ravana. He shot a celestial weapon at Ravana, cutting off his head. But to Ram's surprise, a new head grew at the same place! Ram again struck him hard, but Ravana remained unharmed.

When Vibhishana saw this, he quickly rushed to tell Ram of Ravana's only weakness. Ravana had been given the boon of immortality by Lord Brahma. The only way to kill him was to shoot him on his navel with a *Brahmaastra*.

Without losing another moment, Ram called upon the powerful *Brahmaastra* and aimed at Ravana. It struck Ravana at the navel and he died instantly.

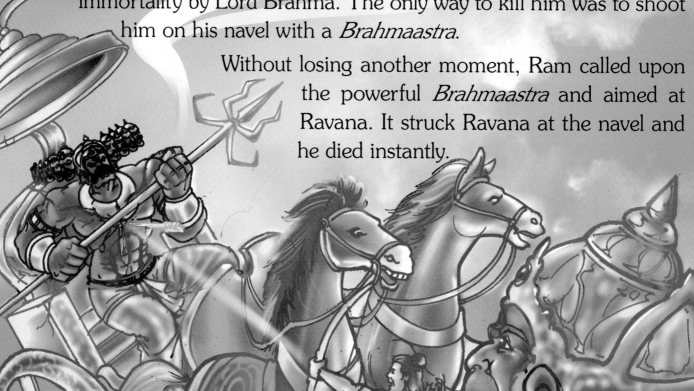

The war was finally over! The monkey army filled the air with the cries of triumph. Hanuman rushed to the Ashoka Garden to inform Sita of the happy news. When she heard it, she blessed Hanuman.

Before leaving the Ashoka Garden, Hanuman wanted to punish those *rakshasis* who had tormented Sita. But Sita asked him to show compassion and forgive them. Hanuman forgave them and led Sita out of the garden.

Vibhishana was crowned the king of Lanka. He made arrangements for Ram, Lakshman, Sita and Hanuman to be flown back to Ayodhya on a flying chariot.

All of Ayodhya rejoiced at their return.

After the war, Hanuman expressed his loyalty to Ram and remained with him for the rest of his life.

Hanuman's Devotion

After Ram's coronation, Ram and Sita decided to give out gifts to their friends who had helped them in their tough times. Hanuman was very dear to both of them. Sita took out her beautiful pearl necklace and gifted it to Hanuman. But Hanuman took it and dashed it on the ground! Sita was very surprised.

She asked, "Hanuman, didn't you like my present?"

Hanuman replied, "Mother Sita, I don't need these tokens to show your love for me. You both are ever present in my heart."

Saying this, he tore open his chest! Everyone gasped when they saw the images of Ram and Sita inscribed within Hanuman's heart! Ram and Sita embraced Hanuman and blessed him.

Overwhelmed Ram said, "Hanuman, my worship will be incomplete without you. You shall always be present wherever my name is uttered."

Sita said, "Peace and plentitude will always follow you."

One day, Hanuman saw Sita applying vermillion in the parting of her hair. He grew curious and asked her the reason behind it. Sita smiled and said, "It is for the well-being of my lord Ram." Hanuman too wanted to pray for the well-being of Ram. So he smeared his entire body with the vermillion powder! That's why even today, the idols of Hanuman are painted red!

Ram and Sita ruled over Ayodhya for a long time. There was peace, love and harmony in the kingdom. The excellence of Ram-Rajya (Ram's reign) remains proverbial to this day.

After ruling for several years, Ram decided to return to heaven.

Hanuman wanted to join him too.

But Ram said, "Hanuman, you are immortal. You shall remain here for as long as my name is worshipped." Saying this, Ram departed while Hanuman stayed back to take care of Ram's devotees.

Glossary

apsara	beautiful supernatural woman
yajnakund	the place for the sacred fire in a yajna
kheer	rice pudding
patal lok	the underworld
swayamvar	practice of choosing a life partner
rakshasi	demoness
rakshasa	demon
vajra	thunderbolt weapon of Indra
guru-dakshina	tradition of repaying the teacher
Lord Vishnu	deity of Hindus
Kuber	God of wealth and riches
Yamraj	Lord of death
Surya dev	Sun God
Lord Shiva	one of the most important gods, he forms part of the Hindu trinity, also known as the 'destroyer'
churamani	crest jewel worn in the hair
Sanjivani	magical herb
Brahmaastra	divine weapon given by Lord Brahma
Panch-mukha	five-faced
Viswakarma	deity of all craftsmen and architects
yajna	sacrificial rite with fire to please the gods